John Russell Hayes

The Brandywine

John Russell Hayes

The Brandywine

ISBN/EAN: 9783337329167

Printed in Europe, USA, Canada, Australia, Japan

Cover: Foto ©Andreas Hilbeck / pixelio.de

More available books at **www.hansebooks.com**

THE BRANDYWINE ❧
By John Russell Hayes
With Illustrations ❧ ❧
By Robert Shaw ❧ ❧

Wilmington, Delaware:
The John M. Rogers
Press: 1895 ❧ ❧ ❧

The Brandywine

"I lie as lies yon placid Brandywine,
Holding the hills and heavens in my heart
For contemplation."

— SIDNEY LANIER

DEAR Stream of Beauty,   famed from olden time,
   Renowned in annals of our early days;
      Stream by whose banks the ancient Indians dwelt,
And on thy waters plied their swift canoes,
And in thy woodlands tracked the fleeting deer,
Wawassan called by those red foresters,
Or *Suspeco*, as other legends say:
Stream on whose shores our fathers fought and fell,
Immortally remembered with the name
Of Washington,   and Wayne, our county's pride,
And glorious Lafayette,   and many more,
Whose memories romantic shall not die,
Forever in our grateful hearts enshrined:

Dear Stream of Beauty,   loved of poets all;
Dear to our Taylor in his ardent youth;
The joyous theme of Read and Everhart;
And sung by him from out the southern land,
Lanier, the lover of all loveliness:

Dear Stream of Beauty, flowing gently down
Among the windings of my native hills,
Gathering from all thy tributary brooks
A richer force, and bearing from far heights
Eternal tidings to the hoary sea!
Thee would I celebrate. O fill my page
With thy soft music, and vouchsafe to grant,
In measurement however small, the power
To picture with a true and loving hand
Thy visionary beauty calm and sweet!

A song of gratitude is mine, for since
In boyhood's hour I rambled on thy banks
And bathed or angled in thy peaceful pools,
My love has been for thee; and later days
Have but enhanced the joy thy presence gave.
Youth's golden years and seasons of delight,
Its happy fantasies and dreamings high,
Were brighter yet for thy companionship;
Thy rocks and shadowy groves, thy daisied fields,
Deep pastoral solitudes and placid vales,
And all the voices of thy hundred hills,
Did speak in memorable accents, rich
With messages from Nature's inner heart.

Among thy sunny meadows first I breathed
The joyousness, the passion that delights
In all the tranquil loveliness and charm
Of field and dell, of tree and stream and sky,
Blue misty hill and dreamy woodland soft,

—9—

"The whispering reeds that line
thy small lagoons"

Life-giving sunshine and the fragrant rain,
The dew-drops twinkling on the grass and leaves,
The billowy clouds,—soft islands of the air,
Morn's tender radiance, and the hushed repose
Of forest sanctuaries, and the songs
Of warbling birds, wild Nature's choristers:
May's vernal freshness exquisitely fair,
The sunny summer-tide of poppied ease,
The gorgeous autumn's melancholy grace,
And all the beauty of the rural world.
How many happy hearts have thus been led
To close communion with earth's lovely forms,
Belovéd Brandywine, and who would not
Record with grateful voice the debt of joy,
Of pure unfading joy and rapture high,
Whose first awakening he owes to thee!

Born of the distant hills and northern woods,
And wandering wide throughout a fertile land,
Bringer art thou of richest fruitfulness,
Abundant harvests and the laden bough.
Full-handed plenty follows all thy course,
And thou art blessed by thankful multitudes
Who love thy placid beauty well, and hold
In fond regard thy ever-winding stream,
Each quiet little gulf and gleaming bay,
From those high crystal springs that give thee birth
To thy last reach in Delaware's far fields.

For whether hastening with murmurous song
Down pebble-fretted slopes, or lingering
In tranquil majesty along thy deeps,
A kindly influence is ever thine.
No fairer meadows or more fertile farms
Are known than those thy quiet currents lave.
Thy mellow acres yield their rich increase
Of clover, corn, and gently waving wheat;
Sleek-coated cattle graze upon thy meads,
The sweetest flowers cluster by thy banks
And waft their incense from a thousand vales.
The old farmsteads upon thy grassy slopes
Are homes of a contented people, proud
To till the acres which their fathers held
Ere that red day on Birmingham's high hills.
Here old-time faith and manners are not dead;
Calm days and nights fill out the tranquil year;
Simplicity hath here her dwelling-place,
And all is pastoral happiness and peace.

Far from hot pavements and the vexing cares
Of crowded marts thy quiet waters flow, —
By silent groves and soft idyllic glades,
By upland slopes where wild strawberries grow,
And meadows green with spicy peppermint;
By banks where bloom the cowslips named for thee,
And fields of crimson clover where the bees
Are gleaning fragrant harvests all the day:
Now loitering many a cool and shady mile

*"Some loud-droning mill
among the trees"*

By woodland aisles and sylvan corridors,
Where moss and tangled fern clothe all thy banks
With softest green, and little fairy groves
Of dainty maidenhair sway in the breeze;
Now drifting quietly in sheltered pools
And fords where mild-eyed cattle seek the shade;
Now issuing forth into the gleaming day
And rollicking with silver laughter down
In foaming waterfalls, across whose breast
The tiny rainbow bends its jewelled bars.
Then winding forth again thou dost caress
The whispering reeds that line thy small lagoons,
And water-grasses whose long amber arms
Wave ceaselessly along thy currents clear.

And oft thy forceful waters are restrained
And sent along the full, rush-margined race,
To turn the mossy, ever-dripping wheel
Of some loud-droning mill among the trees.
What pleasure, pausing here, to peer within
The olden chambers dim with dusty meal,
To see the portly sacks of new-threshed wheat,
And yellow corn that almost bursts the bins,
And hear the mill-wheels grumbling o'er their task
Of grinding grain for all the countryside !

Beneath the arch of many an ancient bridge
Thy waters move with eddying swirl, untouched
By languors of the dusty road above.
In stately march thou sweepest past the fields

"Beneath the arch of many
an ancient bridge"

Where ruddy farmers ply their harvest toil,
Mixing the music of the whetted scythe
With thy soft murmurs, piling up the rows
Of dry, sweet-smelling hay, which thence is drawn
In creaking wagons to the generous mows
Of old stone barns, – upon whose mossy roofs
The crimson-footed pigeons sit and croon
In sober companies; now wheeling down
In white-winged circles to the yard below,
To pick the scattered grains of wheat and oats;
Now settling on the eaves with stately pride
To show the beauty of their burnished necks.
High overhead the snowy cloud-land floats,
And in the mirror of thy lucent depths
Repeats the beauty of its mystic forms,
Its pearly mountains and its creamy capes,
And islands drifting through the azure seas.

How sweet I found it oft on summer days
To launch my boat, and on thy placid tide
To drift as do the clouds, without a care,
And full of peace as they. O hours of dreams,
Of dreams and soft imaginings and fond
Reflections, fantasies without a name!
Or waking from my revery, 'twas joy
To send the boat along with eager stroke,
Rousing thy surface into sparkling rings
That eddied toward the shore with rhythmic dance.
Anon I loved to pause with dripping oar,

"To drift as do the clouds, without a care,
And full of peace as they"

And peering into thy transparent deeps,
To mark the timid fish that hovered there,
The silver-sided chub, the dusky bass,
And little sunfish with their golden scales,
Now winnowing the water with clear gills,
Now darting with a flash of purple fin
Far into watery shades and silent homes
Of willow roots beneath the sedgy bank,
Or shadowy chambers in the sunless rocks.

In drowsy afternoons oft have I heard
The tiny insect voices by thy shores,
The lazy chorus of the katydids,
The faint, small murmur of the busy gnats
That dance in fretful clouds above the sands
That border on thy shallows, and the keen,
Sweet chirrings of the sleepy locust-kind,
Those happy idlers of midsummer days.
There would I muse till misty evening brought
The clear nocturnal croakings of the frogs
Sheltered beneath thy overhanging banks,
Or perched upon green lily-pads afloat
In star-lit waters of thy waveless coves.

The tranquil evening hour beside thy stream,
What peace and pensive solitude then reign!
The herds have left the fields, the harvest-teams
Long since have gone with their last fragrant loads;
Soft vapors o'er the meadows sleep, and all
Is rest and quietude, save where the dove,

In some cool covert hid from human eye,
Grieveth and grieveth all the darkling eve.
Ah, gentle mourner, what soft pain is thine,
What tender melancholy stirs thy breast?
Perchance some old romantic sorrow lies
About thy heart, or memory of wrong
Done to thy kind long since in some green vale
Of dim Thessalian woods. Thy pensive note
No elegy can match, and thy sweet woe
Makes memorable the sacred twilight hour.

An ever-varying poetry is thine,
O gentle Brandywine; songs light or grave,
As fancy's changeful ear interprets them,
Thy crystal-chiming waters sing to me.
Yet not thy voices only do I hear,
Soft and mellifluous ever though they be;
For blending with their harmony the sound
Of Old World rivers comes across the years,
And pleasant revery bears me to the banks
Of Derwent sweet, whose music filled the heart
Of Wordsworth while as yet a little child;
Or silver Duddon, offspring of the clouds;
Or honest Walton's peaceful river Lea;
Or that slow-winding stream, the languid Ouse,
Well-loved of him who sang of country joys
In calm reflective verse; or yet again
To old Dean-Bourne, where by the plashy brink
Grew Herrick's daffodils whose loveliness

"*Thy peaceful charm and sweet tranquillity*"

He made immortal. Yea, and farther yet
My musings carry me, and echoes faint
Of reedy-marged Ilissus do I hear
Murmuring of nymphs and river-deities,
And all the glory of the violet hills
That lie around Athena's marble town.

Athena! ah, the name is here unknown;
Unheard Cephissus and Ilissus here;
Thy woodlands are unhaunted by the nymphs,
No hamadryads whisper 'mid the leaves
Of thy tall trees; nor does the sportive crew
Of satyrs range with Pan thy vernal fields.
No far-descended echoes wake thy hills
Of that poetic life whose perfect joy
Made fair unto all time Aegean isle,
Idalian fount, and Heliconian vale,
And liveth now but in the faded grace
Of carven Attic frieze or Grecian urn.

Nor does the nightingale, lorn Philomel,
Among the shadows of thy moonlit glades,
Pour out her old ancestral threnody
For Itylus through all the summer night.
Nay, yet thy thickets have their own sweet bird,
The poet-bird that keeps his lonely state
In sylvan cloisters far from eye of man,
The dear wood-robin! Underneath green roofs
Of forest solitudes what joy to hear

The liquid fluting of this minstrel rare
Thrilling the beechen shades with rapturous song!
Now fading, now returning, comes his voice,
In purling cadence clear as is the plash
Of sweet-toned rills o'er pebbles smooth and cool.

Streams of romance and beauty have I known, —
The lordly Shannon rolling down his tides
Far in the west of green Hibernia's isle;
The tranquil Thames that dreams beside the grey
And storied walls of Oxford's ancient town,
And passes on through England's loveliest meads
By many a hamlet quaint and flowery garth;
The "wandering Po" that waters Lombardy;
And Rhone's imperial river, icy-pure,
Bearing a largess from high Alpine fields
To pour into the lap of the Mid-Sea.

Yet still with happy heart to thee I turn,
Beloved Stream, that nourished first my joy
In rural beauty and idyllic scenes,
And solitude, that teacher calm and wise.
Well may fair Chester County's children bless
Thy tranquil flood that from far northern hills
Brings fruitfulness to these wide meads and vales,
And fills the fields with verdure rich and deep.
The soul and centre thou of every tract
And fertile township where thy currents flow:
Each bubbling waterfall, each amber pool,
Each tributary runnel dimpling down

"*And those wide hills of storied Birmingham*"

From folded hills, confirms thy gentle power,
Thy peaceful charm and sweet tranquillity.

Unfading is the loveliness that clings
Round each familiar scene along thy course:—
The upland fields of fertile Honeybrook;
The willowed banks of pastoral Fallowfield;
The silent wooded vales of dear Newlin,
Home of arbutus and primeval pine,
And its old hillsides where my fathers wrought
For generations long agone; thy shores
In green Pocopson, haunt of fishermen;
And pleasant Bradford rich with waving corn;
And those wide hills of storied Birmingham,
Where Lafayette, exemplar bright and pure
Of old noblesse and ancient chivalry,
Spared not to shed his blood in our high cause,
And linked his name and Liberty's for aye!
Such beauties and such memories still cling
Around thy valleys and thy verdant glades,
Rich pasture-lands and silent, virgin woods,
Historic hills and loved ancestral farms,
From those high crystal springs that give thee birth
To thy last reach in Delaware's far fields.

Forever fair, O Brandywine, art thou,
Forever fair in thine unceasing flow!
A type and symbol unto restless man
Of calm contentment, and devotion high
To duty's bidding,   with unceasing flow

"Rich pasture-lands and silent, virgin woods"

Fulfilling through the years thy destiny.
The sun in stately majesty doth rise,
Across wide heaven journeys all the day,
Fades in the purple west and disappears;
The sickle moon swims high above the woods
And sheds her radiance o'er the dreaming hills,
While that lone eremite the evening star
Comes loitering across the azure fields.
Each hath his season, each his time of rest:
But thou unresting art; majestic sun
And sickle moon and lonely evening star,
In turn are mirrored in thy lucent breast,
While day and night thou movest on thy way,
Forever fair in thine unceasing flow!

Then blessings on thy heaven-given power
To cheer the heart of man with lofty joy,
With joy and sweet content and deepest peace,
Dear Stream of Beauty,—flowing gently down
Among the windings of my native hills,
Gathering from all thy tributary brooks
A richer force, and bearing from far heights
Eternal tidings to the hoary sea!